THE RAID ON IRAN

Joe Becker

New Publishing Partners
Washington, DC

Published by New Publishing Partners
2510 Virginia Ave,
Suite 702N
Washington, DC 20037
www.npp-publishing.com

ISBN-13: 978-0615575599
ISBN-10: 0615575595

Cover design by Deborah Lange

THE RAID ON IRAN

Joe Becker

Contents

I.

AT KANGAVAR

BRIGADIER BEN-ZEV sat on a rock and waited. The night
air penetrated his field jacket, and he wrapped his long arms
round his chest to stop the shivers. He stared to the West, to the
Iraqi border, 150 miles distant. He would hear the helicopter
before he saw it, he thought, but he strained to see in the darkness
nevertheless. He was not too late, surely. The old Volkswagen,
with Iranian plates, gave out in the sandstorm, a storm that
blanketed the thin band of rocky road running from Qom to
Hamadan, but he had managed to walk the rest of the way. He was
now south of Kangavar, according to plan. The simple, luminous
compass he had bought in a London gun shop last year had kept
him straight.

He rehearsed, again and again, the facts that would go into
the report to the prime minister. The P.M. would read it, he knew,
with characteristic solemnity; he would not panic, as lesser men
might. Prime Minister Abulafia was a Sephardi, the scion of one
of Israel's oldest families, resident in Jerusalem for centuries. His
immense dignity gave no license to panic—or even high emotion.
He would take it all in quietly, with reserve, and turn to Dr.

Wasservogel and General Halkin, chief scientist and chief of staff, for comment. He would then decide.

Ben-Zev scratched the walrus mustache he had grown to pass as an Iranian. Indeed, except for his great height, he looked like one of the innumerable imitators of President Mostofi. He would shave it off as soon as he returned to Caesarea.

Andrea would be waiting. He could not tell her when he would be back but she was somehow able to intuit his comings and goings. She would be sitting on the terrace of the villa looking out to sea, grasping tightly the arms of the rocking chair, waiting, waiting. There was between them still the passion that had compelled her to abandon her husband. She looked at him (he had said to her) the way Bergman looked at Bogart in the last scene of *Casablanca*: unconditional, vulnerable, expectant love. And he was overthrown by that look.

Now he heard the rotors. The copter was low, 100 feet above the road, coming fast from the west, bearing false markings of the Iranian Air Force. The copter caught him in its bottom light and came down. He was in the cabin almost immediately. "Shalom, Brigadier," said a voice. The accent was American.

II

THE RIDE HOME

THE HELICOPTER was a souped-up version of the Kiowa reconnaissance model, a good deal faster and more maneuverable than the prototype, with longer range. The Americans, seated up front, were silent. As the copter reentered Iraqi airspace in its westward flight, the Brigadier settled into a back seat in soporific silence, peering into the darkness. The crew knew better than to speak to him. In a dream state, Ben-Zev mused.

His friends called him the "Parsi," Persian in Hebrew. Family tradition traced his people back to the remnant that did not return to Judea despite the blandishments of the conquering Persian King Cyrus, 2,500 years ago. Remaining in what was to become Tehran, the Ben-Zevs prospered, generation after generation, until emigration to Israel in 1950. They settled in Bat-Yam, a shabby suburb just south of Tel Aviv. Later, Benjamin was born. His first language was not Hebrew but the Farsi of the family. He spoke it with facility; it even accented his Hebrew.

His education was unremarkable until high school teachers began to notice occasional displays of brilliance. He was too playful, too capricious for consistently outstanding work—soccer was his real interest—but, now and then, as when a math problem struck his fancy, he produced work of sterling quality. He entered the Hebrew University, in Jerusalem, quite uncertain about a suitable field of study. *Faute de mieux*, he drifted into the Physics Department; here, he found, he could distinguish himself with little effort. He recalled the moment when he was transformed. Professor Rabinovitch asked him to demonstrate the error in a crucial calculation. Ben-Zev spent the night at it. Rabinovitch looked at his answer the next morning. "I would call this a *Persian* solution" he said, his sarcasm cutting close to the bone. "It is so bad *it is not even wrong!*" Shaken at first, the challenge, mixed with Rabinovitch's wit, confirmed him in his course. He became a serious student of nuclear physics, completing his doctoral dissertation on particle accelerators under Rabonivitch in record time.

He was sent by the government to the Cavendish, in Cambridge, where he spent a year in advanced nuclear work. But military service now called, and, as he had grown tired of college sherry parties, tasteless food, and the bad weather, he was glad to leave. He was directed into intelligence work, focused on the progress of Arab states in exotic armament production, nuclear, chemical, and biological. With his inherited affinities, Ben-Zev was perfectly cast as an observer of Iran's secret program, where a little man running the country was believed to be transforming oil into frightful weapons by a very old process: selling one to buy the other.

Ben-Zev joined a network of agents, military and civilian, dedicated to this work. Some were in Europe keeping an eye on French, German, Polish, and Russian equipment suppliers shamelessly eager for Iranian business notwithstanding sanctions officially in effect. Others, in various masquerades, exposed to great danger, were in Iran itself, feeding information to Jerusalem through channels of the highest secrecy. One such cell, the Zechariah Group, had played a vital role in securing the country and his career in 1981.

Early in that year, Ben-Zev, a young lieutenant then, was summoned to the office of the Chief of Staff. The Chief and Colonel Gaon, head of Mossad, the Israeli CIA, were waiting. The Chief came to the point quickly.

"You are of course aware of Saddam's nuclear research center, al-Tuwaitha." The Chief's reference was to a sprawling Iraqi complex, scattered over ten square miles near Baghdad, where the advanced French reactor Osirak had been installed by the very dead dictator. Ben-Zev nodded. Everyone knew of Osirak. Its shiny aluminum dome was visible for miles.

"We now know," the Chief asserted, "that Osirak is indeed capable of producing bomb-grade uranium. The government has decided that it must be destroyed." He waited to let that sink in. "But the timing of a bombing attack depends on more precise information. We wish to minimize casualties; we must know when the number of operators is minimal. We must know when their anti-aircraft defenses are least likely to be a problem. We are asking that you enter the country and get the facts."

Ben-Zev paused for a moment. "Yes, of course," he said quietly.

"Good. A plan of entry and communication has been developed by the staff. Colonel Gaon will take you through it."

Within two weeks Ben-Zev, with the help of the Zechariah Group, was in and out of Iraq, and the chief of staff had what he wanted. On June 7, 1981, at 6:25 p.m., during the dinner break of the Iraqi aircraft gunners—who had (inexplicably) shut down their radar—and when only a handful of operators were on duty, a sortie of Israeli jets damaged Osirak beyond repair. The mission was the making of Ben-Zev. Promotions followed.

The helicopter lurched, shaking Ben-Zev out of his reverie. He adjusted the tiny flight desk on the back of the front seat and began to draft his report to the Chief. It would be best to get the facts on paper while still fresh. The copter refueled at the American base at Sulaymaniyah in eastern Iraq, and flew on, across Iraq through approved Jordanian airspace. Ben-Zev completed his work just as the Mediterranean came into view in the morning light.

They landed at a small heliport on the coast south of Netanya. An old Mercedes, with driver, waited. On the road to Caesarea, the Brigadier fell asleep.

III

THE REPORT

To: The Chief of Staff

From: Brigadier Benjamin Ben-Zev

Subject: Mission to Iran.

1. At the urging of the American government, I was recently requested to enter Iran, to make contact with the Zechariah Group, and to determine the truth or falsity of the Group's recent reports that the Atomic Energy Department ("AE") of the Iranian government has now succeeded in constructing several nuclear devices for mounting on long-range missiles, perhaps for delivery to and detonation in our country. American support of the mission was crucial.

2. I am able to confirm that the reports of the Zecharich Group are true. I set out below the details of my investigation.

3. The background of the Iranian undertaking to construct such devices is well-known. Since 2004, some 400 tons of uranium hexafluoride (UF_6) have been produced at Isfahan. The UF_6 is feedstock for centrifuges, purchased from Pakistan, at the Natanz enrichment facilities. There, about 3000

centrifuges have spun UF_6 in cascades that increase greatly the concentration of weapons grade Uranium-235 present in the feedstock. The second, more sophisticated enrichment facility at Qom also holds 3000 centrifuges. Both facilities have produced a sufficient quantity of weapons grade 235 to make a total of six missiles. These are of a multistaged solid-fuel type, the Sajjil. It is easily transported, quickly readied for firing, and brings our country within range. Members of our team were able to infiltrate Qom and confirm that the missiles exist and are capable of easy installation on intermediate range launchers.

4. The critical facilities at Qom are deeply underground and invulnerable even to deep-penetration American bombs; that has prompted storage of all missiles at Qom. Destruction of the Qom facilities and missiles will consequently require a commando operation. Such an operation has not yet been defined.

IV

CAESAREA

ANDREA LANDSMAN was born in Ramat Hashavim, an old settlement of refugees from Germany, urban dwellers transformed into chicken farmers. For a long time, these Berliners, Leipzigers, and Hamburgers spoke German among themselves, learning Hebrew slowly and with difficulty, resisting the language in unconscious rebellion, perhaps, against their fate. That phase passed.

By the time Andrea was born, the residents of the settlement were grateful for the lease on life granted them. They had become Israelis down to their toes, passionate and belligerent, living (as they saw it) in a surround of menace. They had done well in their chicken business, moreover, and now lived comfortably, if on guard. Andrea grew up here. She soon longed for action in a wider world. She had been a clever student, and eventually matriculated at the Haifa Technion. She took a degree in chemical engineering—not a field of choice for women—and found a job with a manufacturer of chemical fertilizers near Arad, in the Negev.

As she sat on the terrace of Ben-Zev's villa looking out to sea, she reflected on that period of her life. She worked in the laboratory, trying to develop more efficient phosphoric compounds. She achieved one great breakthrough—a metaphosphate far more effective for plant growth than anything on the world market—but remained dissatisfied, a cloud of depression about her. When she met Yakov Stern, a voluble, wealthy, and sophisticated Tel Aviv lawyer, she saw in him larger prospects; she yielded to his energetic pursuit. They married rather in haste. She soon found that she had not solved her problem: the marriage was agreeable and sexually passable (no more), and she was well cared for. There were no children. Nor was there passion.

How different it was with Ben-Zev. She longed for his return. She heard the key in the lock and rose, turning to the door. But she remained on the terrace. When he entered the apartment he saw her immediately. Her face gave his heart a turn. It was always thus.

"Shalom," he said. No more.

"Hello." This from the terrace, still keeping her distance. The sight of him traveled through her like an electric current.

"How are you, darling?" he asked.

"Better, now." She moved no closer, keeping control. He heard the tremor in her voice.

"Have you had a hard time?"

"Yes. But I somehow knew it would be today." She noticed the silly, bushy mustache and remembered that he had grown it for the mission. It gave him a cruder look, she thought, obscuring the elegance of his nose and mouth. "Are *you* all right?" "Fine, fine." He put down his frayed leather bag and strode to her. "Dear one," he said, taking her in his arms. It was her mouth that awoke him to life, an astonishing sweetness that he experienced only here. They held each other for several moments. She stepped back.

"Are you really all right? Let me see you. No wounds or scars. Nothing went wrong?"

"Nothing went wrong."

"Good. *Baruch Hashem.* Thank God. Good."

They separated now, and he looked around the room, familiar yet unfamiliar. Too many books crowded the wall. She had wanted to move most of them. It was a project, like many others, that went undone.

"I'm hungry."

"I knew you would be. Will you take an omelet and tea?"

"Perfect."

She kissed him once more and moved to the kitchen. The phone rang.

"It will be for you," she said, as she busied herself.

"They know I'm back." Ben-Zev picked up the phone. "Yes," he said.

"Brigadier," said the hoarse voice of Halkin, the Chief of Staff. "*Baruch Haba*. Welcome. Good to hear your voice."

"Thanks, General."

"Are you OK?"

"Yes. Just tired."

"Of course." A respectful pause. "When will you be ready for my courier?"

"It's ready now, General, if you will take it hand written."

"Excellent. Lieutenant Zahav will be there in an hour. You know him. Give it to him. I'll call later about a meeting. Get some rest. Thanks." The Chief rang off.

He ate quickly, silently, as she sat opposite him at the kitchen table, watching. She did not know why or where he had gone, or what he'd accomplished, and knew that she must not ask. Sometimes he told her a little but he would not do so now; the subject was supremely confidential. His fatigue betrayed an ordeal. She rose and, in the bedroom, turned down the bed, knowing that he must sleep some before the inevitable meeting in Jerusalem.

"Give this to Zahav when he comes," he said, handing her the envelope. With that he fell into bed.

Later, after Zahav had come and gone, she slipped into bed beside him. Half-asleep he clumsily pulled her to him. Her familiar scent roused him, a triumph over his fatigue. Within moments they were joined to each other. They both then fell asleep. When the phone rang again he knew the summons to Jerusalem had come.

V

THE PRIME MINISTER'S OFFICE

THE OFFICE of the Prime Minister was spartan. The desk, chairs, roundtable, couch, and bookcases were in walnut, giving off an air of dark seriousness, relieved only by the bright blue and white flag standing in the corner. The shelved books seemed to be reference works: the *Encyclopedia Judaica*, the *Encyclopedia Britannica*, dictionaries in Hebrew, English, and French, and official statistical works published by governments. Histories of the Jews and (a more recent interest) of the United States were also to be seen. One shelf was dedicated to works of history in French. Prime Minister Abulafia, born 52 years earlier in a house a few blocks from his office, was alone, his desk clear except for Ben-Zev's report. His handsome, darkly semitic face, usually cheerful, was saturnine. With his left hand he stroked his chin, as if shaping an invisible beard, a gesture characteristic of his old teachers at the Yeshiva. He had come a long way from that school but its mark was ineradicable: it had turned him into a professor with a sentimental (if unexpressed) attachment to the faith of his fathers. Unlike his predecessors, generals and apparatchiks all, he had come to his office from academic life, a renowned historian of the Mediterranean and the surrounding Sephardi communities, an intellectual legatee of Fernand Braudel and the College de France. An international reputation for scholarship and integrity preceded him into the political life.

That began just a few years ago. He was transformed by the Intifada from dove to crow (if not hawk) and rose to prominence in a series of public debates in which, with quiet certitude and eloquence, he charged opponents of the left and right with mindless disregard of the real interests of the nation. To his surprise, he was elected to the Knesset on a centrist ticket—he would gladly cede sovereignty of the Temple Mount but would not permit the return of long-departed Palestinians—and, to his astonishment, became the leader of a coalition that enabled election to the Prime Minister's office.

Abulafia turned to the business at hand. He did not know Ben-Zev except by reputation. Halkin spoke highly of him, as did Wasservogel. His report demanded action. But the P.M. was not quite sure of the course he must take. He would await the views of the Chief of Staff and the Professor before reaching any conclusions.

The phone rang. "They are here, Prime Minister," Mrs. Solomon informed him.

The group filed in. Halkin and Wasservogel were no more cheerful than he. Ben-Zev was expressionless. They arranged themselves around the conference table.

"*Chaverim*," the P.M. said softly. "Friends." Although he knew of the daring achievements of Ben-Zev, he offered nothing in the way of flattery or special recognition and merely said, "I'm glad to meet you, Brigadier. Are you well?" He betrayed genuine avuncular concern here.

"Yes, sir," Ben-Zev said, stiffly. He had seen the P.M. on TV and, once or twice, at formal military reviews. Close-up, he was even more impressive. Ben-Zev, remembering Trollope from his Cavendish days, thought that, if Israel had a nobility, Abulafia would be the Duke of Omnium. That neither was an Ashkenazi resonated, unspoken, between them.

"Perhaps the Brigadier will be kind enough to summarize the position," the P.M. said quietly. The gravity of the subject was lightened by this polite formulation. It was a style the P.M. acquired unconsciously as a student in Paris, a style rare in the tough school of Israeli politics.

"Mr. Prime Minister," Ben-Zev replied in kind, "my visit to our neighbor has convinced me that they are in possession of nuclear missiles in a state of launch-readiness. I observed the warheads myself. They are surprisingly sophisticated devices, constructed out of imported and home-made materials. They display considerable technical skill, far more skill than I believed they possessed. The Ph.Ds they educated in America seem to have paid off. Funds have been applied on a lavish scale to the importation of critical elements."

"I'm afraid that the Brigadier is right, Prime Minister," Wasservogel interjected. "I've gone over the ground with him. His conclusions are sound."

For the P.M., this endorsement of Ben-Zev infused his report with credibility. The P.M. did not know Ben-Zev but his trust in Wasservogel's scientific judgment, based on years of academic association, was unshakable. Wasservogel was to Abulafia what Lindemann had been to Churchill.

The P.M. turned to Halkin. "Sir," Halkin said after a long pause, "you are well aware of the risks. The fanatical tendency of President Mostofi and the government in Tehran may well prompt them to carry out their threats as soon as they are able. The Americans oppose preemptive attack, but we must move. We have, by the way, sent them Ben-Zev's report, as agreed, and thanked them for their help in getting Ben-Zev in and out."

"I wonder, gentlemen, how Mostofi regards our retaliatory capacities" the P.M. asked. His implication was plain.

Dr. Wasservogel jumped in. "Knowing what we do about his past intentions, we must assume that he believes that a powerful strike will preclude a response. Recall our operations in Iraq and Syria."

Ben-Zev remained silent. He was, in this group, a mere brigadier. As it happened, he agreed entirely with Wasservogel. Abulafia did not fail to notice his body language of assent.

The Prime Minister reflected. Wasservogel was not alone in holding this view. The political and military risks of a commando raid were of course grave. The risks to the soldiers themselves were obvious. The consequential military risks to the state were enormous. And the possible effects on international relations were incalculable: some in Europe would be furious. The fact remained that Israel was the prime target, and Abulafia could not, would not, contemplate fatal damage to his country, whatever world opinion might be. And, after all, there was the Osirak precedent. Israel had received private congratulations for that operation from governments all over the world.

Almost at a whisper, he said to Halkin, "Yes, General, a commando operation had occurred to me and, indeed, you will need to plan such an operation most carefully. Start on that immediately. We will meet again when you are ready. Meanwhile, the relevant ministers must be informed and the political risks assessed. How much time will you need?"

"Prime Minister, we cannot let more than ten days pass. We will impose that deadline."

"Good, gentlemen. Let us adjourn to another day. Thank you. And thank *you*, Brigadier, for your extraordinary work."

VI

LIEUTENANT ZAHAV

LIEUTENANT YOSSI ZAHAV—once Joe Gold, a literal translation—was glad the long day was over. He headed for his Ford Escort, parked in a privileged spot on the lot of General Halkin's staff. The envelope he had delivered to the Chief, he knew, was important but he was trained to suppress all curiosity in such matters. Although he was, for the moment, seconded to the office of the Chief, he well knew that his real work was running a commando unit with headquarters on the northern border. He would doubtless be ordered back soon.

Joe Gold had grown up in Brooklyn—in Flatbush—an ordinary kid among ordinary kids, playing stick-ball and touch football according to the season. His parents, survivors of the Holocaust, had little to say about that horrific time and lived a life of contradiction: disabused of belief in a benevolent, omnipotent God who permitted—what else could one conclude?—Auschwitz, they nevertheless enrolled Joe in a day school where he was taught to pray in and speak Hebrew in the morning and to learn math and American History and English composition in the afternoon. He was very good at English composition, middling at everything else.

That competence moved him in the direction of a career in English literature. But in his junior year at CUNY, in the midst of courses on Shakespeare and American Lit and Joyce, Proust, and Mann, he was swept up on an afflatus of feeling that he belonged only in Israel. To the astonishment of his parents, he quit the college and fled, as it were, to Jerusalem where, after a short interval, he—now Yossi Zahav—joined the Army, the IDF.

He completed basic and advanced infantry training, was sent to commando school, became expert in the use of explosives—he was able to blow up targets, large and small, with the precise detonative impulse necessary—and distinguished himself on more than one tricky mission to Syria and Lebanon. Officer Candidate School followed. For the moment a mere cog in the wheels of the office of the Chief of Staff, he awaited his next serious assignment.

He swung the little Escort in the direction of the Hotel Gilead on Jabotinsky Street. Most nights, it was at the bar of the hotel that he joined a group of regulars in the pursuit of beer or, better, Scotch.

The Gilead was a small, run-down hotel that, inexplicably, became an attraction for Russian immigrants recently arrived. Handsome women from Moscow and Kiev, and other centers of what remained of Russian-Jewish life could be found at the bar. Yossi and his pals came to drink, to relax and, perhaps, to get lucky.

In that department of life Yossi had advantages over others. Not the best looking, Yossi was more intellectually sophisticated. That was currency that he could exchange here at favorable rates. Young women were delighted by him, and access to the hotel's rooms after a few drinks was a real possibility.

Yossi parked the Escort up the hill from the Gilead and walked down to the hotel. He arrived as the last rays of sun flashed over the horizon.

Several of his buddies were there, well advanced into drink. It pleased Yossi to join the scene. The familiar voices, the familiar joshing, the familiar debate about the Palestinians, the familiar speculation about the accessibility of the women, all of that warmed him.

"Yossi," several shouted at once. "Come, sit, have a beer. Tell us what you did today to save your country."

The truth was that, unknown to him, he had done a great deal.

"Nothing, absolutely nothing," he answered. "I'm the Chief's favorite errand boy. I can't wait to get back to the Galilee.

I've got a platoon of commandos up there getting stale, losing discipline without their favorite lieutenant to keep them straight." He asked for Johnny Walker Black, on the rocks, rather than beer.

"You'll be back soon enough" said a sergeant, a much-decorated veteran. "And you'll not get decent Scotch there."

"True, too true," said Yossi. He gulped the whisky. "But at least I'll not have to listen to the same bullshit every night. I'll be too busy saving my ass."

Out of the corner of his eye Yossi noticed the not beautiful but arresting face of a dark young woman in her twenties seated at a corner table, speaking animatedly to an elderly gentleman. Yossi had seen the fellow somewhere before. He was not military. The woman he did not recognize. When, by chance, their eyes met he was sure he'd struck a chord.

As he turned away, he remembered the old man. It was Professor Wasservogel, a frequent visitor to the office of the Chief. Looking again, he saw the resemblance between the girl and— surely—her father. To get at the girl he would need to address the great Professor, who might not have any recollection of him. Yossi was too aroused by the daughter to worry about the father. He approached the table.

"Hello, Professor Wasservogel, how are you?" No recognition. Hasty addition: "I hope you remember me." No eye-contact with the girl.

"I'm sorry, I—oh, yes, yes, you work for the Chief of Staff. Lieutenant Zahav, is it?"

"Yes, sir. I just thought I'd say hello. I'm surprised to find you in this dump."

"Oh, my daughter and I meet here once in a while. This is she." He pointed. "Devorah, this young man works for General Halkin."

Devorah looked up at him. Smiling, she said, "you're an American."

His accent had given him away. Hers was deep and guttural, the real McCoy, he thought. "Yes, I'm afraid so. A latecomer."

"We forgive you," she said. "In America you say better late than never, don't you?"

This was kind. Although she was seated, Yossi could hardly fail to notice the excellence of what her simple dress displayed. As Wasservogel finished his drink, Yossi said "I hope you have a ride home, Professor." It occurred to Yossi that he was pushing it.

"Of course, my driver should be waiting."

"What about you, Ms. Wasservogel?"

"I live here, Lieutenant, just a few blocks away."

"Good," said Yossi. "Then I shouldn't disturb this father-daughter reunion. My friends are waiting." He was about to back away when Wasservogel spoke. "No, I was just leaving for the office, Lieutenant. Will you see Devorah home for me?"

This was perfect, thought Yossi; paternal approval. "Sure. I'll just finish my drink." The Professor rose and left; Yossi took his seat.

Devorah looked at Yossi with more than passing interest. The fellow had a glorious smile (it was a male version of Julia Roberts's), reinforced by eyes of robin's-egg blue. His gestures were broad, playful, American.

"How long have you lived in Jerusalem?" Yossi asked.

"It's been years, now," she replied. "The family lived in Haifa but I came down to university and simply stayed on."

"So you work here?"

"Yes, yes." She stopped short, and he sensed a reluctance to go into detail.

"I suppose it's a burden to be the daughter of the great Professor Wasservogel."

"Sometimes it gets in the way. Most people see me on my own terms. I'm not complaining. But tell me about yourself."

Yossi gave her the short course on his American origins. But when she pressed him about why he'd come to Israel, he said that it was an emotional thing that he could hardly explain to himself. In any case, he was here, for good. As she listened to him she began not to listen but to attend to the movements of his mouth and felt the gravitational pull of his body. She needed to escape.

"I really must go."

"Sure. Let me walk you."

They set out together. It was a short walk to her apartment on Marcus Avenue. They shook hands, awkwardly. He said, "Hope I see you again." She nodded.

VII

MR. POWERS

JOE POWERS—JOSEPH Augustine Powers, to be precise—
waited in the outer office of the Prime Minister's suite. He had
been sent by the President, at the request of Abulafia, to listen to an
Israeli plan of which he knew almost nothing.

Powers was Deputy Director of the CIA. He had joined
the Agency in the midst of a promising career teaching law at
Columbia. He was not sure why he had suddenly, in the middle
of a term, resigned from the faculty to accept appointment to the
utterly different office he now held. Partly, no doubt, it was to
rekindle, at a more intense level, the old friendship he once had
with the President when they were both Alabamans at Princeton.
He acknowledged, too, that teaching the basics of corporation law
had lost its charm. Whatever; here he was, shifting uneasily in the
August heat in a brown, rumpled seersucker suit that amused the
locals.

It was his first trip to Israel. While he knew a good deal about
the Middle East (privy, as he was, to the darkest secrets of the
region), Israeli politics were not—he had to admit—clearly in
focus. The internal affairs of the country, the deadly in-fighting

within and between parties in the struggle for power, were beyond him. Foreign policy was easier. Beleaguered countries made similar moves.

"More coffee?" Mrs. Solomon was doing her best.

"No thanks, ma'am," Powers drawled. The last word seemed to have several syllables.

"You are enjoying our weather?" she now asked.

She had to be kidding. "Well, ma'am, it's about as bad as Alabama in August. Jerusalem is drier, I guess."

The President had called before he left Washington. "Joe," he said, "this is important. Pay attention. You've seen the Ben-Zev report. Come see me as soon as you're back."

Powers's reverie was interrupted when Mrs. Solomon said, "He will see you now, sir."

Powers knew faces. Abulafia's was a good one, he thought. Someone had said that, after forty, a man gets the face he deserves. Abulafia must have been a good man.

"Please, sit down, Mr. Powers. I've brought you all this way for a most important reason."

"I assumed as much, sir."

"Yes. Of course." Amused by the soft sounds of the American South, the Prime Minister rose from his desk and walked slowly about the room. He formed the next sentence deliberately.

"I believe you know, Mr. Powers, that it is the policy of Israel, reiterated by our various governments to your presidents over the past 40 years, that we would not allow an enemy to develop nuclear weapons capable of deployment against us.

"Yes, suh. We do know that."

"You, of course, remember the initiatives we took in 1981 and again in 2007."

"The whole world knows about Osirak, suh. And of the operation in Syria."

The P.M. now recounted in close detail the Ben-Zev mission and the resulting report. Powers kept silent throughout.

"We cannot," the P.M. finally said, "allow the present state of affairs to continue."

Powers knew what this meant. He paused. "Mr. Prime Minister. You understand that I'm not now in a position to comment substantively. There is this, however: we have our own concerns about Iran. How your conduct might affect those plans is something we must consider."

"Yes. We understand that. But there is urgency for us that does not press on you. The issue is now the central concern of my government."

"I appreciate that, suh". Powers paused. "I don't know what the President will say. He may wish to avoid a premature blow-up over heah."

Abulafia moved about the room silently, stopping to gaze out the window in the direction of the Western Wall. After a long silence, he turned.

"Mr. Powers. From this window I can almost make out the Western Wall, the vestiges of our temple that stood here 2000 years ago. The Wall is sacred to us. It stands as a reminder of what Jerusalem once meant and what it means to us today. I will not preside over its destruction. Tell the President that this is raison d'état in its truest sense. The mission must go forward." Powers sensed the gravity of the moment. He was moved. But he yielded nothing.

"I take it that your plan takes into account a possible retaliatory response." Abulafia turned from the window. "Of course. Two things should be kept in mind. The Iraqis did not respond to Osirak, knowing our capacity to do *very great* damage in further response. Nor did the Syrians. Tehran must also take that into account. That capacity we still have." Abulafia looked meaningfully at Powers here. "Whether they are reckless enough to risk that kind of response is an unknown, of course."

The P.M. took his seat behind the desk once more and went on. "The question for the President, Mr. Powers, is not whether he approves, for we must go through with this thing; the question, rather, is whether he is prepared to support our effort in ways that can be developed. We would of course welcome that; we leave it entirely to you."

Powers reflected. He could say nothing. Then he said, "I take it, Prime Minister, that you will not move for 72 hours in any event. I return to Washington today. You will hear from us in due course."

With that, Powers shook hands and left.

The flight back to Washington was as fast as could be managed. Within the hour of his arrival, Powers was in the Oval Office.

"They will certainly go ahead, Mr. President."

"You can hardly blame them, Joe. Nor am I sure we should try to stop it. Knocking out their nuclear capacity in one go does us a favor even if only for a few years. Time is then on our side."

"That's true, suh. But if Mostofi answers with what he has left–a conventional missile attack–and Abulafia responds in kind, or worse, the whole region would light up. I don't think we're now ready for that scenario."

The President was silent for a moment. There was between these two Alabamans and college buddies an extraordinary ease.

"It's possible that Mostofi will do nothing, of course. The attacks are pinpointed after all; it's not a general attack."

"I don't know, suh. It means the loss of nuclear military power. They must save face before an agitated people, after all."

"Well, let's get the boys and girls together on this and see how it plays. Get them all in the Situation Room in an hour."

In the Situation Room there was remarkable consensus. Some cautioned that it would mean the end of the tilt to Islam. But there were no doves. The extreme hawks saw the Israeli raid as an opportunity, finally, to impair or knock out a reckless government: if they attacked Israel in response, the U.S. would cut loose all the air power still in the region. The moderates in the room, although divided, saw the issue in simpler terms of loyalty to an ally. The President was urged to go for it, but not to signal his intentions to anyone.

Three hours later, the Secretary of State instructed the American ambassador in Jerusalem to visit the Prime Minister and tell him that the United States will simply await developments.

VIII

CAESAREA AGAIN

BEN-ZEV WAS GRANTED the day off. He needed rest. In the early morning light, looking west, he could see the beach from the terrace of his house. The waves now washed over submerged Roman ruins. Caesarea had been the capital of Herod the Great, the surrogate of Rome, the friend of Marc Antony. It was now the home of an Israeli upper class. The wheel of history had turned.

"Let's go for a walk," he said to Andrea.

"On the beach you mean?"

"Yes. Exactly."

"Good. Let me just change my shoes."

They walked quickly, eager to reach the water. At this early hour, except for a dealer in antiquities just opening his shop, the life of the beach had not yet begun. They had bought a Phoenician glass vase in the shop a few weeks ago. Like the Romans, the Phoenicians too had vanished from the Land of Israel.

"*Boker Tov, Adoni,*" came the voice of the dealer. "Good morning, sir. May I be of service?" The voice emerged from the darkness of the shop, not yet lit by the morning sun. They looked in. It was the usual stuff. Some of it fine. Some of it junk.

"Have you anything new and special?" asked Andrea.

"A little ceramic bird just came in. Roman. Quite lovely."

"Let's see."

The shopkeeper, in carpet slippers, shuffled to a drawer. He unwrapped a stylized eagle, dark red glazes, black breast. Late Roman, she thought. Fine piece.

"Oh!," she exclaimed; she held it to the light, smiling, handed it to Ben-Zev.

He, too, thought it delightful but, not wishing to show his hand, said, merely, "Nice." Then, "*Kamah*? How much?"

"Oh, not too bad, *Adoni*. We are reasonable."

An eagle was about right, he thought. He would be flying off in a few days. An appropriate gift.

Andrea turned to look elsewhere.

"Darling," Ben-Zev said. "Let me do this. It's lovely." He turned to the dealer, haggled, and there was agreement. The shopkeeper wrapped the bird in paper, put it in a box. They turned to go.

"*Todah rabbah*," said the shopkeeper. "Thanks a lot."

Andrea embraced Ben-Zev as they left. "*Todah*, my love," she whispered. They walked on.

"You do look tired, my darling" she said, seeing him now clearly in the bright sunlight. He knew he must go back. He did not mention this or the reason he bought the eagle.

"I'll be fine in a day or two. This is what I need."

With that, alone on the beach, with their feet in the surf, he embraced her, finding her mouth once more. It had a sweetness that he could recall in no other woman. He wondered: was this cause or effect? Was it *because* she tasted so that he had been drawn to her or was it the *effect* of their love that made her taste so? This was the kind of puzzle that amused the ancients— appropriate in Caesarea—but was foolishness now.

They had met at a dinner party a year ago. One of the grand old ladies of Tel-Aviv society, the widow of a biochemist who had done important work at the Weizmann Institute, had invited Andrea and her husband, Yakov, and a mixed group that included Ben-Zev. There was much talk of the American war on terrorism post-Afghanistan, of settlement with the Palestinians. Yakov, a lawyer animated by drink, once a graduate student at the Harvard Law School, did most of the talking. He claimed to understand the American mind.

Benjamin said very little. He was not much interested in speculation in the absence of facts. He saw the world through the eyes of Sancho Panza, not Don Quixote, believed in evidence, facts, reality. He was reminded of his old grandfather from Tehran who met all political events with the question, "Is it good for the Jews?" Benjamin's *Weltanschauung* was wider than this but only in degree. Besides, he had been trained as a scientist, impatient with the disorder of politics.

There was something else to explain his silence. Benjamin had noticed Andrea. He had more than noticed her. The old Beatles song from his days at the Cavendish came to him: "Got to Get You Into My Life." He was surprised by the vividness of her presence; he felt it in a peculiar, biological way. A current of jealousy of Yakov ran through him; and it was this (he later realized) that had thrown a blanket of silence over him.

The next day, when Andrea received his phone call inviting her to lunch at the King David in Jerusalem (which she accepted), she recognized that he had shaken her in some undefinable way.

The time with him at the restaurant passed quickly, and they moved rapidly into the realm of personal revelation.

"But, then, you cannot love your husband," he found himself saying. They had come very far indeed.

"I admire him very much," she conceded.

"That's not love."

She said nothing in reply.

"Then why are you here?" he asked, pushing his luck.

"I've asked myself that. It's something to do with your voice. I wanted to hear it again."

That was not quite what Benjamin expected. He had missed its import. For Andrea had made a profound admission, only half-understood: to miss a voice is to miss a whole being. Speaking softly as much to herself as to him, she added, "I just couldn't stay away." The politics of sex were not her forte.

Benjamin decided to go for broke.

"Look," he said, "I've got to be back at the office. But I can be free in a couple of hours. Will you meet me here at the hotel at four?"

She nodded.

Andrea went off to an art gallery she knew on the Lincoln Road, paused to look at a painting by Reuven Rubin, and wondered whether to shop for shoes. Her extraordinarily narrow feet were hard to fit. She dwelt on that quotidian thought to avoid the reality that loomed. Too agitated to shop, she circled the old YMCA building. When the Bloomfield Garden—just below the hotel—

came into view, she crossed King David Avenue and found a bench where she might catch her breath.

A bridge had been crossed too. Andrea was frightened at what she'd agreed to do. She should go home. But she could not. He was, strangely, already present.

She entered the busy lobby of the King David a few minutes after four. He was not yet in sight. Andrea took an unobtrusive seat in a corner and waited. If he did not come in five minutes, she decided, she would leave.

Benjamin entered just then. He was promptly recognized by the receptionist; his old exploits in Iraq were well known. Andrea noticed a transaction of some sort between the two. Benjamin turned, spotted her, approached, took her by the hand, and with that irresistible voice said, "Come with me."

She offered no resistance. They entered the elevator. Silence. Off at the third floor. Silence. Key in the door. Open. Enter. Shut. Silence. He led her to the bedroom.

Sitting on the bed, she suddenly said, "I can't. I just can't."

Benjamin stopped. The soldier knew he now faced a problem in tactics. He had moved too quickly. To storm these defenses would surely fail. He sat quietly beside her. He would move to the flank. Touching her face gently and turning it to him, he kissed her softly. No more.

"Oh, God," she said.

There was in this little cry the beginning of the end. The soldier knew the wall had been breached. It was not, for him, a question of seduction, or, at least, not merely that. Andrea had moved him more than he thought possible. It was now *her* voice that he longed to hear.

"Dearest lady," he said, and kissed her once more, gently.

She yielded at last, put her arm on his shoulder and drew him to her. "You are too much, Benjamin, too much for me."

They had now fallen across the bed and were pressed together. She felt his member through her skirt. Impulsively, with uncharacteristic daring, she touched him there. They now kissed ferociously. The absurd wrestle with clothes began. At last they were able to join. "My darling," he finally whispered.

Each now knew, like a jet pilot breaking the sound barrier, that they had entered a new realm, a world from which there was no turning back.

Two months later, Andrea abandoned Yakov and moved to Caesarea.

All this passed through her memory as the two walked the beach.

"Shall we have coffee?" he asked. He pointed in the direction of the beach restaurant, now open for business. "Lovely." They climbed up the sandy path, found a table with a view of the sea, and motioned to the old waiter.

As they sat in perfect silence looking at the waves, Benjamin said, "I must go back. I'm sorry."

Andrea put her cup down slowly, not looking up.

IX

THE PLAN

THE OPERATIONS ROOM of the office of the Chief of Staff
was a beehive. Senior officers poured over maps and computer
printouts to settle on a plan, answering pointed questions about
men, terrain, equipment, contacts, weather, military positions.

Brigadier Ben-Zev was not an expert in these matters—he
was a physicist with experience in intelligence (he reminded
himself)—but a number of points seemed clear to him. The force
must be small, as small as possible, with competence in combat,
communications, and the setting of explosives. He envisioned
entry by helicopter, landing close to Qom, at night, followed by
hasty departure by helicopter from a nearby rendezvous point. For
the moment, he merely listened.

There was disagreement. While all asserted that, after the
blow-up, speedy exit by air was essential, other points were in
doubt. The Americans, with bases in eastern Iraq, must again be
asked to help.

Disagreement centered on the mode of entry. In the balance
were considerations of speed weighed against likelihood of
detection.

"It's a run of 300 miles from the Iraq base. The copter must be large enough for the team."

"What about one of our smaller transports, flying in low?"

"No reliable airfield and tough at night."

"And their radar can't be dismissed."

"Commandos from the Galilee?"

"Who commands?"

"Zahav."

"You're kidding. He's too junior."

"He's junior. But he's superb and experienced with explosives. Remember him in Lebanon." That was a particularly successful demolition job Zahav had done.

"How does the Brigadier fit in?"

"He knows the layout and the targets."

Ben-Zev nodded. "I'm just along for the ride, gentlemen."

"What's the jump off?"

"Sulaymaniyah. Into Iran south of Samandaj, past Hamadan. Down to the site at Qom, at night of course."

"The Guard?"

"Ben-Zev must deal with our man. He'll think of something."

The reference to "our man" was meaningful only to a few in the room. The others knew it was not their business.

"That may blow his cover."

"We'll take him with us if he wants. Ben-Zev will tell him. In any event, we're ready for a fire fight."

And the exit?"

"What's the weather?"

"Good for the next week. But sand storms at the site are likely. That has advantages."

"What explosive?"

"The Brigadier has proposed a small nuclear device. It will not only blow the site to pieces. The radiation will end future use of the place as an underground facility. Of course, we'll be gone before the blow."

The Chief of Staff, who had been firing most of the questions, pondered. There were risks he would not mention. But the general plan made sense. "All right," he said. "Get it on paper. Distribute to the key players. Wait for the P.M.'s order."

Ben-Zev, recalling Macbeth from his Cambridge days, thought, "when 'tis done, then 'twere well it were done quickly."

A young computer mavin in the back of the room, Corporal Gross, took this in. The information was worth a price, he thought.

X

ABADAN

MAJOR GENERAL BASIL Abdullah sat at a small table in a dark corner of a filthy cafe on a back street of Abadan, at the southwestern corner of Iran, almost touching the Iraqi border. The refineries could be seen from where he sat. The heat made Abdullah doubt he had chosen a good table. He was, moreover, impatient. The General wore shabby clothes of the city. He was unknown here. The citizens of Abadan would not have been interested in him. Abdullah was waiting for someone.

He knew nothing more. Ahmed would identify himself with the torn top of a box of "Majestic" coffee; Abdullah held the other half for the same purpose. Ahmed was to bring a message.

General Abdullah found himself in this curious position because of a decision made immediately after the disaster of the war with Iraq. Then a colonel of infantry in a regiment that had fought well, Abdullah watched the destruction of the army in horror. He was nevertheless heroic in defense of his sector. The President decorated him for that. He was sometimes seen on television sitting at a long table among other officers, wearing mustaches and military berets, in parley with the leaders. Only

Mostofi appeared to speak. The others sat silently, like tin soldiers arranged by a most careful child.

Advancement did not diminish Abdullah's fury at the government, which he labored to contain and disguise. The casualties on the retreat, the disgrace of it, the loss of friends were unforgivable. His anger had slowly evolved into treason to the regime. To the *regime*, he thought, not to his country. In his new frame of mind, Abdullah was uncertain about next steps. His inner rebellion was far too dangerous a subject to share with fellow officers. Mindful of the gruesome fate of the German generals who set out to assassinate Hitler, Abdullah's heroism did not embrace suicide.

Abdullah learned of, and was led to the Zechariah Group, a few Israelis secreted at the Iraqi border. Abdullah had furnished them with useful bits of information. Now, it appeared, the Israelis had something special to ask of him and were sending Ahmed to ask it.

As he downed a second cup of thick coffee, he was approached by an unshaven, grizzled, limping old man carrying a large suitcase. He had entered the café moments before, and appeared, at first, to be a traveling salesman of trinkets.

"Blessings upon you, sir," the old man said.

"And upon you," Abdullah replied cautiously.

"May I be seated, sir?"

"As you wish."

Carefully easing himself into the chair opposite, the old man said, "I believe I have something of interest for your eminence." With that, he removed from his case a leather-bound, elaborately tooled copy of the Koran and handed it to Abdullah. The General opened it slowly. Just after the first sura, *Fatihah*, he found a book mark of sorts, the torn half of the top of a box of Majestic coffee. The General leafed through the pages and placed at the 104th Sura — the last — the matching half.

"I'm afraid I'm not interested in the Koran," the General said. His ancestors, an ancient sect of Christians that had gotten their theology wrong, were now a fragmented minority.

"Pity, sir, pity. A rare bargain."

The old man now drew himself up. He was plainly not as old as he made himself appear. He spoke softly.

"My name is Ahmed. I bring you a message of importance: our friends will soon come to destroy the 'second facility.' They ask whether you are willing to assist."

General Abdullah was taken aback. Such an operation at Qom would deal a great blow to the government. But the dangers, risk of failure, were enormous. The risk to himself, successful or not, would be equally great. Nor was he sure that he could help.

"What do they wish me to do?"

"The operation will be conducted by a squad of commandos. Their means and time of entry and exit are unknown to me. As the operation is through your command, they ask that you assist their safe passage. They will send an intelligence officer to brief you."

The General reflected. There were too many unknowns.

"Tell our friends this," Abdullah said. "I will not move unless the whole plan is put before me. I must speak directly to the officer in command." He avoided the word "Israeli." "Tell them I'll be in Athens the day after tomorrow, on mission: at the Prince Edward Hotel. Their officer will find me there as Mr. Houdoon. He must have the other half of this bill." With that, Abdullah tore a 1,000 rial note into rough halves and slipped one to Ahmed. "And he is to carry an Egyptian passport."

"I will tell them, sir. They will be in touch."

With that, Ahmed locked his case and limped away.

XI

DEVORAH

DEVORAH WASSERVOGEL walked to work. Her line of march took her up Marcus Avenue to a kikar—a traffic circle— where a left turn put her behind the Van Leer Institute. There, in a small building of concrete blocks, hidden from view by a stand of *arbor vitae*, she put in ten hours or more a day.

What she did was known only to her father, the professor, and to her colleagues: top secret planning for special units of the Israel Defense Forces. Trained in mathematics, masterful in the uses of computers, she was invaluable to the Chief of Staff.

Devorah knew all there was to know about the imminent commando raid. That Brigadier Ben-Zev must be in the party was obvious. That Zahav, a mere lieutenant, would be in command of the demolition squad was not. That surprised and disturbed her. As she sized up Zahav at the Gilead, Devorah had no doubt of his competence. Though it was unclear what disturbed her, disturbed she was.

He had telephoned twice since they met. Yossi not only liked what he had seen but admired what he heard. She was brighter than he (he admitted) but far more serious. Her intelligence fairly sparkled on the phone; that magnified his attraction. Besides, she had a great body. Like phone sex, their conversations roused him to tumescence.

That evening they would meet for dinner and go on to a concert at the Music Center. Yossi knew he would be embarrassed: his tickets were not for adjacent seats; he would sit directly behind Devorah.

"Have you been to the *Dagim* before," he asked. He had chosen a fish restaurant on the Keren Hayesod.

"No," she said. "But I'm pleased to know it. The fish nets on the ceiling are a nice decorative touch."

She added: "I don't get out much; late hours at the office. There's so little time. It's wonderful to be able to do this."

"What *do* you do?"

"Oh. Clerical stuff for the Agriculture Ministry." This was a much-rehearsed line.

"And they work you hard *there*?"

"You'd be surprised."

They were silent for a moment.

"But you. What are *you* doing in Jerusalem?", she asked.

"Temporary assignment. Someone at the top thought I needed exposure to the chief's style. I don't know why. But I'll be back with my unit in the north soon."

Devorah knew this, as she knew most things about his immediate prospects. She feigned innocence.

"And what happens there?"

"I run a company. Special forces. We do our share."

Devorah knew that too. She was uneasy, holding unfair advantage in this conversation.

"I hope you're looking forward to the concert. It's mostly Mahler."

"Mahler's grand. Do you know which?" Devorah asked.

"The Fourth, I think. The one with a soprano in the last movement."

"Yes, that's the Fourth. Wonderful."

The conversation sped along easily. They knew many of the same things. But Devorah knew more. It unnerved Yossi. As they rose to leave, he noticed her bottom. It was an excellent bottom.

For her part, Devorah was conscious of excitement. She was not greatly experienced in these matters. In her student days, she, unlike her classmates, avoided affairs, doing math with zeal, remaining shy and aloof. And she had indeed been working late hours, limiting her social life. It was clear that Yossi was not going to be a casual acquaintance. The smile she noticed at the Gilead was now often present, and it delighted her.

At the concert hall, Yossi took his place behind her; both were amused by the incongruity. The high emotion of the Mahler served only to intensify feelings running back and forth between them. Yossi wanted to speak to her but it was awkward. At last, he wrote on the back of the program, "We are going to be important," and handed it up. She entered the simple endorsement, "Yes," and returned it. They sat in silence through the enthralling last movement.

They were silent on the way back to Marcus Avenue, a joint unease in the presence of the numinous. At her door, Devorah turned to thank him. In the instant, he drew her to him and kissed her, deeply. Inexperienced as she was, she responded without calculation, holding him to her. To gain purchase, he placed a hand on her buttocks, pressing her in. In this close communion, she was alarmed: she did not wish to feel this intensely. And as she knew he was about to embark on a most dangerous mission—about which she could not speak—she trembled.

Yossi knew they had both come very far. He said, "I'll call you tomorrow." She answered, "good." She knew that tomorrow he would be gone.

But the next day, toward evening, the phone on her desk rang. "Hi. It's me," he said. The anonymity of the opening presumed intimacy.

"Where are you?"

"I'm not in Jerusalem, I'm on the way to the Galilee. We've stopped for a moment. Sorry about this."

"You've been ordered back, haven't you?"

"Yes. That's it. I didn't know yesterday."

"And when do you move on?" It was an idle question, for on reflection she knew the answer.

"I can't say." The ambiguity was necessary, Yossi thought.

After a moment's silence she said, "Well, look, tomorrow's Shabbat. If I drove up to, say, Tiberias, could you meet me at the Blue Beach at noon?" She surprised herself with this initiative.

"Yes. I know the Blue Beach. That should work. But I won't have much time."

"That's o.k. Can you do lunch, at least?"

"Probably."

"Grand. See you then."

As she put down the receiver, Devorah admitted that this was remarkably pushy behavior on her part. "What's going on?" she wondered. She had just offered to drive for hours on Shabbat (her day off) in the hope of spending a moment or two with this guy Zahav, whom she hardly knew. It was extraordinary. She was flying, she thought, by the seat of her pants, a metaphor (she saw with amusement) that located precisely the impetus of her conduct.

Yossi, for his part, was cheered by the prospect of seeing her again. His orders were incomplete—he was told simply to return to his unit and await further instructions—but rumors were rife that he would be on a raid in a matter of days. He wanted more time with her, to confirm what he suspected, that they had indeed found each other. He would find a way to be in Tiberias, and the Blue Beach, at noon.

The circuitous drive from Jerusalem to the Galilee—west, north, east—made the journey tedious, a tedium compounded by heavy traffic (an offense to the orthodox on Shabbat). But the Galilee itself, when she reached it, presented lovely vistas, the Lake, the final reward of her labors. She reached Tiberias just before noon, drove north to the Blue Beach, parked at the obvious lot, and waited.

At last, she saw Yossi, running. He moved with marvelous grace and agility, an avatar of youth. She leapt from the car, waved, and they ran to each other. They embraced.

"How was the drive?" he asked, for lack of anything more inquisitive.

"Fine. Fine." It was no longer relevant. He was supremely relevant now.

"Are you hungry?" he asked.

"Starved."

"Good. There's a little bistro I know on the corner. Moroccan cuisine. Yes?"

"Of course."

As they walked, he held her arm close to his side, almost lifting her. She felt at one with him. At the *Epices*, he ordered spiced lamb, she a St. Peter's fish. They ate quickly.

"How are the troops?", she asked.

"In better shape than I thought they would be."

"Bored?"

"Some of the time. But the terrorists keep them on their toes. They infiltrate and shoot up civilians. Or they lob shells over. No suicide bombers lately."

"How do you respond?"

"We give chase. We shoot back. Sometimes we nail them." He shrugged.

"When will it stop?" she asked no one in particular.

"When they've had enough. I don't think they can go on much longer."

"It's the irrationality of their demands that depresses me. We can't possibly take back all those refugees from 1948. It's absurd." She said this with an air of fatigue. Changing the subject, coming to the point, she asked, "How much time have we?"

"About an hour. I thought we'd walk about the Lake."

On the shore, they ambled. Yossi skimmed pebbles on the Lake surface. The sun illuminated the water magically. Entering a cave, a sheltered nook of the Lake, they were quite alone, hidden from land and sea by trees and shrubbery.

They sat on a patch of grass. Devorah noticed a fallen leaf on his shoulder and reached, protectively, to brush it off. He caught her arm, kissed her, and they reclined. They gazed at the sky. There was so little time. She would not wait; she rolled on to him. Moved by instinct, without experience, she grew more fervent, kissing deeply. Yossi was with her: he unzipped and was between her legs. She wanted this. Yes, she wanted this. She helped. At last, they were at rest. She lay quietly upon him. Neither moved.

In her romantic delirium, Devorah—who was unprepared for the event—hoped she would bear his child. "I love you," she said, "and there's nothing for it." He smiled at her. "Me too, my darling."

XII

ATHENS

THE PRINCE EDWARD Hotel in Athens was not very princely. It was, it is true, an immense pile, located on Constitution Square, in the heart of Athens, across from the old Parliament building. But heavy air pollution from passing vehicles had darkened its once alabaster walls, and, while a certain dignity prevailed within, it called to mind lesser nobility, the residence of barons perhaps, not dukes. It was here, in a suite on the fifth floor, that General Abdullah had immured himself.

That morning, Cyprus Airlines flight No. 02 from Nicosia brought to Hellinikos airport, Athens, an Egyptian businessman, Abdal Mossuf. That, at least, was what his passport stated under a photo of a dark, mustached Semite. He cleared customs easily and told the cab driver to take him to the Prince Edward. The driver said that his meter was out but that the usual fare was 40,000 drachmai. That was an inflated, preposterous lie. His passenger said he would pay only 15,000 drachmai. The driver pondered: "20,000," he said. "Very well," said the passenger. This was, after all, Athens.

At the registration desk, the clerk offered room 620. Brigadier Ben-Zev would not accept the first room offered, and asked for something else. He took room 430. Bugging was less likely in a room unforeseen.

He checked for wires; the room was clean. He immediately called the desk and asked to be connected with Mr. Houdoon.

The clerk said that Mr. Houdoon was out but would be back that evening. That was not a misfortune. Professor Wasservogel had told Ben-Zev that, for reasons the Professor could not disclose, it would be helpful if Ben-Zev would bring back from Greece samples of water of the river running by the village of Agia Marina, up the coast from Athens. It was a foolish diversionary request given the importance of Ben-Zev's trip to Athens, but scientists, he knew, had different perspectives on the world than other mortals.

Agia Marina was not much of a place: a handful of olive growers and their trees. Ben-Zev turned to the driver and asked (in English) to be taken to the river. The driver understood not a word.

This was embarrassing. Ben-Zev knew no Greek. He was stuck in a car with an uncomprehending driver who had simply been told to take his passenger to Agia and return. The delay in sorting this out could cost him the meeting with General Abdullah.

Pondering his position, Ben-Zev rattled his brain. How does one say "river" in Greek? Some English words derived from Greek, he recalled. Did not "hippopotamus" mean "horse of the river"? Surely, the "hippo" part meant "horse," as in "hippodrome," where horses raced. The "potamus" might be "river." He tried it on the driver: "potamus," he shouted. The driver smiled. They were off. They reached the river in no time. Ben-Zev collected samples in Wasservogel's bottles, much pleased with himself. They returned to Athens in good time.

Immediately after he entered his hotel room, Ben-Zev phoned Houdoon's room.

"Yes," room 510 answered, in Farsi.

In Farsi of equal authenticity, Ben-Zev said, "I've arrived from Egypt, Mr. Houdoon, sir. I look forward to seeing you. Room 430." That was all.

Abdullah told his security guard that he was visiting a lady in the hotel and should be back shortly. Minutes later, in room 430, the two exchanged matching halves of a rial note, introduced themselves, and sat down to coffee.

"General," Ben-Zev said, coming to the point, "this is our plan. You must tell me whether the part we ask you to play can be performed."

Ben-Zev proceeded to describe how six men and equipment, in a helicopter at night, would enter Iran from Iraq within a mile north of the site at Qom, enter the nuclear facility through an underground fire exit, do their work, and run for the helicopter. The question for Abdullah was this: as commander of the area, could he reduce to a minimum the troops they might encounter?

Abdullah kept silent through all of this, smoking a small cigar. At last, he spoke.

"Brigadier," he began. "Your intelligence is faulty." He explained that the proposed landing site was unsuitable; he suggested another.

Ben-Zev was surprised. Accurate intelligence was his watchword.

"Will that field work?" he asked.

"Yes, I think so. It has just been cleared and firmed up by the Army."

"All right."

"You will travel at night, of course."

"Yes."

"Troops at the landing site should not be a problem. The normal disposition of troops there is thin. I can ensure that it will be even thinner."

Ben-Zev nodded.

Abdullah, muttering almost to himself, went on. "The march south will present difficulties."

"How so?"

"Normally, you would run into a heavy concentration of armored infantry here." (Abdullah pointed to coordinates on the map spread between them.) "They are in fixed positions. The concentration increases as you approach the facility. I could move them south for an exercise, say, but— you understand, Brigadier— there will be an investigation following the incident and such a movement of troops would draw suspicion to me with—let us say—unpleasant consequences."

"Is there an alternative?"

"If there were time, a swing north, around the troops, would reduce the risk, but not by much. No, I don't think you can afford that. Besides, you want to enter by way of the fire exit, which I approve. That is in the south, here (pointing). It is normally guarded by a platoon."

"Yes, we knew that General."

"I'm afraid I'll have to move them, Brigadier. That means I'm finished in Iran. I will have to come out with you."

"General, we have planned for that if you want it. You will be safe with us, and we will arrange a new life for you. Have you family?"

"No, fortunately not."

"Then it will go easily."

"Perhaps."

"Are you prepared to do this?"

General Abdullah pondered. He rose from his chair and stood at the window, overlooking Constitution Square. He noticed the density of the traffic and the black emissions from the exhausts. He reflected (drawing upon his cigar) that abandonment of his country was a small price to pay for the destruction of the facility. If it brought about the fall of the government—a possibility—it was a trivial price. And—who could tell?—that might make his return possible.

"Yes. It will be done." After a pause, he continued. "Understand that an order removing all troops would arouse immediate suspicion. Some must be left in place. You will have to trust to speed, caution, firepower, and luck."

"Yes, sir." Ben-Zev was genuinely respectful now.

"Then let us settle the schedule."

The two generals now defined the timing of the operation almost to the minute. They were satisfied that their movements would be synchronous.

With that, Abdullah rose. The two generals shook hands formally, and Abdullah returned to his room. Ben-Zev packed, to catch an early flight to Istanbul and, from there, to Ben-Gurion Airport.

XIII

CORPORAL GROSS

ODED GROSS was a computer wonk. His discovery of the machines in high school, at Petah Tikvah, came as a revelation. Suddenly, after aimless wandering through classes, doing careless work, engaging in brief, unsatisfactory friendships, he discovered his gift for rapid-fire manipulation of keyboard, monitors, icons, modems, software—the whole apparatus. He now spent his waking hours staring at a screen, calling forth hidden treasures from the deep.

He became a hacker. It pleased him to break into coded communications of the government, to disrupt private exchanges, to destroy libraries, to exercise new-found powers. While he made no friends in person, he made a few in chat rooms. Once, he arranged a meeting with an equally dissociated young woman whom he met in this way, but found, at the *moment critique*, that he could do nothing with her.

When he was called to military service, the Army discovered his skills. Things began to look up. He was transferred to key communication centers in Jerusalem and, in due course, to the military intelligence branch. His superiors knew an eccentric when they saw one—he was not a *mensch*, they agreed—but neglected to consider that he was unfit to keep confidences where confidences were stock in trade.

Oded noticed that secrets of consequence passed across his screen or were discussed within earshot. With his eye on the main chance, alienated (as he was) from army comrades and the historic claims of his country, he reflected that there were those who would be glad to pay to know what he knew. The current example was this planned raid on a nuclear facility in Iran. He brushed off the notion that these were treasonous thoughts.

Oded learned that in the Moslem Quarter of the Old City, on Antonia Street, a tobacconist named Gamel had long been a link in the chain of communications of Hamas, the terrorist gang. The Israeli intelligence services could have, but did not, shut down Gamel: unknown to him, they had tapped into his lines, knew what he was up to, and learned more about Hamas than he did about the IDF. Oded thought Gamel could lead him to higher-ups.

Visiting the shop, Oded, plainly an Israeli even out of uniform, motioned to Gamel to join him in the alley, away from bugs that were surely in place. Gamel, suspicious, turned up the volume of a radio on which there was singing (as usual) of disaster. Oded whispered. Gamel said nothing. Then he said, "Tomorrow, 11:00 a.m. at Herod's Gate. A car will pick you up. Good day."

At the appointed hour, at the Gate, he was approached by two Arabs who motioned him to follow. And old Mercedes waited. They drove off, east, past the Rockefeller Museum. Avoiding roadblocks, they entered the parking lot of the Church of the Vini Galilaei, parked, and waited. Nothing was said. Soon, a truck loaded with vegetables pulled alongside. The passenger exited the cab and entered the Mercedes. He was gray-haired, in his fifties. Oded thought he had seen the face before.

In accented English, he said to Oded, "Who are you, young man?"

Oded, nervously, answered, "I'm a corporal in the Israel Defense Forces. Here's my ID."

The interrogator examined the card. "And what is it you wish to say?"

"I have information of great value to the right people."

"Who might they be?"

"President Mostofi."

The interrogator smiled. "And how would a corporal (no less) come by such information?"

"I'm assigned to the office of the chief of military intelligence. I'm a computer technician."

The interrogator now took a more serious view. "And what do you wish to tell the President?"

Oded had rehearsed the next answer. "I can provide part of the information now. Soon, I will be able to supply the balance, the critical balance, which I do not know today."

"Let us then hear the first part."

"Understand this. I will require a total payment of $100,000, cash in hand: $25,000 for what I will now tell you. The rest when I've told the rest." As he spoke, Oded recognized his interrogator as a top official of the Palestine Authority. The name still escaped him.

"I'm not in a position to agree. I can tell you that in a day or two. I suggest you state the first part of your information now. Its quality will determine what follows."

Oded took a breath. "OK. I would inform the President that his nuclear facility at Qom will be destroyed very soon, in a matter of days. That is all for now."

His interrogator looked grave. "We will need a good deal more to justify the expense. Here is a telephone number. Call at precisely 1:00 p.m. tomorrow from a public call box. I will simply say "No" if I have no further interest. Otherwise, I will give you instructions. Good day, Corporal."

Oded was driven back to Herod's Gate and deposited there.

The next day, the answer to Corporal Gross' phone call was, yes. He was to appear the following day at 2:00 p.m., this time at the Damascus gate. Was he ready with the missing pieces? "Yes," he said. At the Gate, the same monitors picked him up. They drove to the Augusta Victoria Hospital. His interrogator of yesterday reappeared and handed Gross a brown envelope, bulky with its contents. Gross looked within quickly and satisfied himself that $25,000 was there.

Gross now recognized his interrogator; he was Ahmed Husseini, of course, deputy chief of Hamas.

"Well?" said Husseini.

"A commando squad will enter from an American base in eastern Iraq in about 48 hours. They will helicopter to a recently cleared field near the facility at Qom. They will blow-up the missiles and return as they came."

"Anything else?"

"They may have an accomplice in the Iranian army of senior rank. That's all I know. I may have specifics tomorrow. I will expect the balance then."

Husseini, without a word, turned and left. He needed no more.

Gross' monitors ordered him back into the car. To his surprise, they now drove eastward, deeper into the West Bank, in the direction of Jericho.

Gross was reported AWOL from his unit the next day. His ditched body was found the following month by a passing IDF patrol. He had been shot once, through the head, at close range. The brown envelope was not in his pocket.

XIV

THE PRIME MINISTER

IT WAS Prime Minister Abulaffia's habit to rise at 5:30 a.m., to fix his own breakfast while his wife slept. He puttered about the kitchen in slippers, boiling an egg, toasting bread, boiling water for tea, not coffee. The process relaxed him. He thought of the schedule ahead. This was the day on which he must decide. The Minister of Defense, the Chief of Staff, and Brigadier Ben-Zev would soon be waiting for him. He was quite sure he would say yes if they were ready. He wondered whether the hypocrites at the U.N. Security Council would again condemn Israel as they had for Osirak. At least the world now knew what the Tehran government was. The Attorney General said it was a case of anticipatory self-defense, arguably sanctioned by the Charter. Be that as it may; it had to be done.

The water came to a boil and he popped the egg in. His aide arrived with the morning papers. Abulaffia glanced at the headlines.

He consumed the egg and toast with pleasure, washing it all down with Fortnum & Mason's Assam Tea, a luxury he permitted himself; he went to some trouble to get it from London in leaf, not bags.

Soon, he was dressed and ready to go. He was a handsome, but not a vain, man. In his youth, he could recall, he was something of a ladykiller. He was well past that now. He looked in on his sleeping wife, fixed her blankets, and left. His limo and security vehicles were waiting.

At the office, the conversation with the group moved forward rapidly.

"On the whole, we think a sandstorm may be a blessing." The Chief of Staff was explaining the final plan. "The Persians are likely to stand down during a storm."

Abulaffia remained expressionless. "Surely, General, the plan does not depend on an act of God. He is sometimes indifferent to the Covenant."

General Halkin was unamused. "Sir, the plan does not *require* a sandstorm."

The P.M. changed the subject. "And you're using a different landing site?"

"Yes. The Athens meeting produced that."

Ben-Zev nodded.

"What do we know about the new site?", asked the P.M.

"Not much. It is firm. The aerial photos are reassuring."

"Will we run into their troops?"

"Probably. We're dressed as their regular army. They're not too bright. If there's occasion to talk, Ben-Zev will do the talking. Small units we can handle ourselves. We'll have to avoid large units."

"Are the Americans cooperating?"

"Within limits. They will let us use their Iraqi base."

"When do you jump off?"

"Midnight. In 48 hours."

Prime Minister Abulaffia turned to the Minister of Defense. "Anything to add?"

"No. We're ready."

The Chief of Staff sensed that the cross-examination was over. All waited in silence.

"All right then. Go. Let's hope *He* is with us," said the P.M., pointing upwards.

XV

TEHRAN

"THE PRESIDENT has the Palestinian information. We are to add a battalion around the facility. General Abdullah has his orders about the area of expected entry."

This was Tehran, and the Chief of Staff was talking. He had been given the story told by Corporal Gross to the agents of Hamas.

His subordinates sat about nervously. Since the Iraqi War, they were gun shy. The Chief could see their unease. He did not lessen their fears; each was under suspicion. He did add, voice raised, speaking as much to himself as the others, "We *must* stop this Zionist operation." The threat was plain. He added, "It will not be difficult.

"Dismissed," he said, impatiently.

Meanwhile, General Abdullah considered his position. The President had telephoned. Oscillating between threats and expressions of confidence, he demanded that Abdullah destroy the Israeli invaders. Abdullah reassured him. Hearing that the wrong landing field would be reinforced, Abdullah was pleased; Hamas had transmitted the old plan, pre-Athens. He was sure, however, that Mostofi would suspect him of treason and that, if Ben-Zev succeeded, his life was forfeit. Nevertheless, he pretended to arrange his troops along a reasonable defensive perimeter—except that he left a gap through which, he knew, Ben-Zev's squad would pass.

President Mostofi wondered about Abdullah. That he was not a Moslem was not in his favor. That he seemed at times cool to the revolution raised a question. But that he was a superb commander, demonstrated in the Iraq war, could not be doubted; none of the others could be counted on.

Mostofi feared the Supreme Leader, a religious fanatic who would not tolerate failure. Mostofi had been installed by him as President in a feat of electoral legerdemain, and he would not hesitate to remove him in that event. Besides, Mostofi shared his fanaticism on the Israel question: the land had been stolen from the Palestinians, Moslems who shared the destiny of Islam.

The Supreme Leader asked whether the missiles at Qom, now ready for firing and tipped with nuclear warheads, could be used even before the Israeli attack, in a kind of preemption of their own. Mostofi said that would take a few days to assemble. The Supreme Leader ordered that this be readied.

XVI

ENTRY

THE AMERICAN BASE at Sulaymaniyah, in eastern Iraq almost at the Iran border, was not much. The helicopter was waiting, however, its few lights visible in the night. The Israelis boarded quickly, with their equipment and weapons. Ben-Zev carried the small nuclear device that would demolish the Qom facility forever.

The route east, approved by General Abdullah, took them at a low altitude past Sandandaj and Hamadan. The copter rotors, they hoped, were out of earshot of any ground troops; none in sight, but the darkness left them uncertain. The danger they were in was evident in their sobriety, a change from the usual horseplay.

As they neared the Saveh-Qom road they spotted the field. It had been cleared of trees and shrubs and packed down. Using the powerful bottom light, they came down, landing softly. The troops disembarked in moments.

Finding the back road that would take them down to Qom was not easy. Although he had visited the Qom facility days before, Ben-Zev had not seen the area before. In the darkness, he made one or two false turns, retreating when he discovered the error. The boys in the rear were not cheered.

At last, Ben-Zev ordered a right turn that, he was sure, was the road marked by Abdullah. But Zahav suddenly ordered a halt. In the dim light, about the length of a soccer field ahead, there was a glimmer.

In the dead silence, a dozen ears now listened with the intensity of radio-astronomers attending to the music of the spheres. Voices. Local Farsi. Possibly a unit of troops. Abdullah had said he could not get rid of everyone. These might be strays he'd left in place.

Lieutenant Zahav said, matter-of-factly, "We will have to take them out."

Ben-Zev was unsure, but this sort of thing was not his call, Brigadier or no. Zahav was in charge of the security of the mission, not Ben-Zev.

Zahav and his squad moved forward almost on tip-toe, crouching, Zahav in front. He saw an irrigation trench running along the side of the road. The squad entered the trench and inched ahead. At 50 meters they could see a road block, doubtless manned by two or three soldiers. Only one was moving about. The others were probably dozing in a pup-tent they had put up.

Zahav spoke quickly: "I go for the guy standing, with my silencer. Shachar and Levin (two tough boys from Russia) will hit the others. Knives should do. *Sheket* (quiet)," he insisted. All now inched forward.

The trench was muddy, Zahav kept losing his footing. He was worried about falls and noise. "L'at. L'at" (slowly, slowly), he whispered.

When he was ten yards from the standing Iranian, Zahav rose, took careful aim, and fired once. The silencer worked. At the same moment Shachar and Levin charged forward and jumped two soldiers dozing in the tent. Zahav's shot was true, penetrating the back of the head of the target, who fell (indeed, was thrown) forward and down without a sound. Shachar and Levin made short work of the other two. Zahav had the bodies dumped into the trench, together with their equipment and the pup tent. A passer-by would not have known that a checkpoint had stood there. "It's done," he said to Ben-Zev, hardly looking at him.

They were now in open desert. In the southern distance, the sound of working oil rigs was audible. The wind began to pick up; it soon began to howl: a dust storm, predicted by Abdullah, Ben-Zev recalled. The sand was blinding. Fitted goggles were put on.

Zahav ordered a halt. They must wait. This would throw off the schedule.

Ben-Zev considered that the storm would oblige any Iranian troops—whom they would surely meet as they neared the facility—to take cover. He suggested that Zahav use that advantage. They would move on as best they could, *now*.

The unpaved road would eventually take them up a slow 10 meter rise. At the top, the fire exit to the facility should be found. A tunnel would take them down to the assembly plant. Ben-Zev did know this leg of the road.

Suddenly they came upon a bunker surrounded by sandbags. Guards were inside. Hearing the commotion, one emerged to see what was up.

"Who the hell are you?", he shouted, shielding his face from the wind.

Ben-Zev stepped down and, in easy Farsi, shouting above the din, said, "Did you not get the signal?"

"What signal."

"That we were coming through."

"Don't know what you're talking about. Wait here."

The guardsman turned and disappeared into the bunker. He emerged a moment later with an officer. The latter said, angrily, his face irritated by the flying sand, "What is this?"

"We had a complaint about the fire exit. Repair crew. Headquarters said you would be informed."

"Well, we're not informed. Let's see your orders." The wind made talk difficult.

"Just a moment." Ben-Zev returned to the squad. To Zahav he whispered, "We can't screw around with this."

Zahav mumbled, "If we hit these guys, we have to do the whole bunker. OK."

As Ben-Zev stepped forward, he slowly opened an envelope, catching the attention of the two Iranians. Zahav also moved forward. The blowing sand blinded the Iranians to Zahav's right hand, which carried a machine pistol. As Ben-Zev moved forward on the left, Zahav, on the right, aimed and fired. Both Iranians fell, silently. Zahav motioned to Levin, who came forward with a single grenade. He went half-way round the bunker, found the steel door, threw it open, tossed in the grenade, and slammed the door. A small explosion rocked the bunker, muffled by the wind of the sandstorm. Levin opened the door and saw that it was unnecessary to fire; the three occupants were slumped over, quite dead.

Zahav shouted, "Let's go." He reflected that, with the wind up, the explosion was probably not loud enough to arouse other troops in the area. The group proceeded, looking for the rise that would lead to the fire exit. Entry through the fire exit should avoid enemy troops guarding the main entrance at the surface.

XVII

ENTRY AND EXIT

IN THE HOWLING wind and sand, the fire exit was not
immediately visible at the prescribed coordinates, but Ben-Zev's
instincts in such matters were sound, and, after moments of
uncertainty, he directed the squad to a rise in the terrain. At the
top, two giant steel doors, angled at 30 degrees to the desert floor,
appeared. No sign of enemy troops; Abdullah again.

Locked from the inside, the doors of the fire exit were easily
blown by a simple plastic charge. The squad now began a tip-toe
descent down a flight of stairs, Ben-Zev and Zahav in the lead.
A tunnel of several hundred yards yawned. The construction
was shabby, resembling a hastily-cut coal-mine shaft. Some
illumination was supplied by caged bulbs of low-wattage strung
along the roof; several were dead and unreplaced. The roof trickled
sand down on the heads of Zahav and his squad with each step.

Ben-Zev recalled that the facility took the shape of an
underground tennis racket: the tunnel was the handle; the assembly
plant, the oversized head. The plan contemplated that, at the mid-
point of the handle, the squad, wearing gas masks, would fire
paralyzing gas into the assembly area. Those guards who were able

to escape into the handle would be hit by the squad. The rest were dehors combat.

At Zahav's signal, the gas bombs were fired and exploded in the assembly area. Immediate chaos followed and, then, silence. Three soldiers escaped, staggering for the fire exit. They were gunned down by Zahav and Corporal Shachar.

Ben-Zev now moved forward with Shachar and Levin. Ben-Zev carried the crucial device. The others covered. As they entered the assembly area, Ben-Zev recognized the scene. The missiles, as before, rested on carriers but were now tipped with nuclear devices, ready to go. Ben-Zev's device was placed where it would be most destructive; it would be fired by radio signals from outside the facility. Satisfied with the work, Ben-Zev ordered withdrawal. The squad dashed for the fire exit.

When they reached the field, a safe distance, Ben-Zev simply said to Corporal Nissim, "OK." Nissim turned on his transmitter, found the frequency, and beeped the signal. An immense roar could be heard. A fireball shot down the tunnel and out the fire exit. The device had worked. The roof of the assembly area collapsed, the facility was a ruin, enveloped in radiation.

The Israelis ran for the copter, an Iranian platoon in pursuit, firing wildly. As Ben-Zev was about to enter the copter, he suddenly crumbled, hit.

Suddenly, a jeep with a lone driver appeared out of the desert. Zahav was about to open fire when he saw the driver, a general: Abdullah, of course. He was coming out with them. Abdullah jumped from the jeep, and asked for Ben-Zev. Zahav pointed. Abdullah saw that Ben-Zev was in bad shape. He greeted him quietly in Farsi: "Brigadier, you disappoint me." Ben-Zev yielded a poor smile.

The helicopter took off, carrying a gasping Ben-Zev. Within minutes, it was heading home.

XVIII

EPILOGUE

BRIGADIER BEN-ZEV did not survive the flight home; he expired of his wounds just as the copter entered Iraqi airspace. When the news reached Andrea, her grief was overwhelming. After months of inconsolable despair, she was persuaded to return to her husband.

Lieutenant Zahav was awarded the nation's highest decoration. Devorah attended the ceremony. Soon thereafter, they married.

Prime Minister Abulafia was widely acclaimed at home. An emergency session of the U.N. Security Council produced furious debate, the Chinese ambassador joining the Arab states' condemnation of the attack. The United States pushed for an equivocal resolution that both justified and condemned the attack.

The world waited for an Iranian reaction that never came. The destruction of the Qom facility encouraged the simmering opposition to Mostofi. He was assassinated by his chief of staff. There now emerged a moderate military group, a triumvirate of generals that took power with promises of eventual democratic rule. General Abdullah was invited to return to his post and did.

ABOUT THE AUTHOR

A graduate of the Harvard Law School who taught
and practices international law, Joe Becker engaged
in large transactions in Iran and Israel that are
sources for this work of fiction. He is based in
New York City and has published widely on legal
subjects.

Made in the USA
Charleston, SC
12 December 2011